RAGE

PROTECTOR
BOOK 1

NORA ASH

TRIGGER WARNING

Please note: This serial installment contains dark subject matters that may be triggering for some.

Specific themes are: *torture, abuse, violence, slavery and sexual assault.*

ABOUT THE AUTHOR

Nora Ash writes thrilling romance and sexy paranormal fantasy.

Visit her website to learn more about her upcoming books.

WWW.NORA-ASH.COM

ONE

AX2

"Activate."

Bright light floods his vision as consciousness returns. Mechanized beeping follows, and then the acrid, familiar smell of disinfectants.

And *her.*

His body tenses on blind instinct, muscles engaging as a snarl rips from his throat. But he doesn't move to follow through on the threat; he has learned not to.

"Temper," she warns him, unfazed, over the tapping of her fingertips over keys. "You will be pleased to know your body has fully healed during stasis. Your vitals are perfect."

Pleased. He breathes evenly. In. Out. He holds the exhale until the sinking sensation of despair fades to numb indifference. This is not unexpected. Every assignment they send him on, every time he feels his body rip apart, he falls into unconsciousness with the faint hope that this time... this time, even *she* won't be able to bring him back.

Every time, he wakes in the stasis chamber. Whole. And tasked with a new mission.

At least there is comfort in the predictability.

"How long?" he grinds out.

"Just five days this time. Faster than we anticipated, considering the damage. Any pain?"

"No."

She taps on her keyboard. The light searing his retinas finally dims, allowing his pupils to dilate enough to take in his familiar surroundings.

The stasis chamber is as sterile as the lab beyond: white walls; a chair and a desk with a computer for her; a steel table and glass cylinders, tubes, and needles for him; and the mirror.

"Sit up," she commands.

He obeys instantly, though the lack of pressure in his brain tells him she hasn't activated his chip. She rarely needs to anymore.

He stares blankly at his own reflection as she moves from her chair to his side to detach the many tubes from his body. The mirror has been there since day one—hung on the wall, where it is the first thing he will see once he has been given permission to sit up.

In the beginning, he felt horror at the reflection staring back at him. They brought him back from the brink of death, he's been told. Made him better. Stronger. And as a result, skin fused seamlessly with silvery metal, giving the appearance of a creature neither human nor machine.

Now, though, there are no visible hints of the engineering that went into crafting the U.S. Military's strongest soldier. Artificial skin covers gleaming alloy, allowing him to blend in with the general population when out on assignment.

Not that it matters—he knows what he is underneath his human facade: something less than a person.

So does she. "Stand."

Once again, he obeys her command without hesitation. The concrete beneath his feet is cool, every unevenness in the surface sparking along his hyperaware nervous system, just as every detail of the stasis chamber and the lab beyond lodges in his brain as he scans his surroundings.

"Eyes straight ahead," she snaps, unexpected irritation flaring in her voice. She rarely offers any emotional response around him, her demeanor always carefully dispassionate, crafted to provide no added stimulation as he returns from stasis.

AX2 flicks his gaze forward. "Yes, ma'am."

She huffs as she steps close enough that he can feel

her body heat against his skin—both artificial and real—and any curiosity her minor burst of annoyance may have awakened in him withers to dust.

Focusing on nothing but his own slow breaths, he stares at a point on the wall above her head. When she brushes her palm over his bare chest, he wills his body to remain still, even as a tremor works its way through every nerve ending she touches.

He has learned to endure pain during his training. Exhaustion. Defeat. Endless exposure has forged the soldier they sought—unbreakable, even under torture.

But this?

This is the one weakness they have not been able to carve out of his flesh and replace with steel.

In. Out. His chest moves under her soft hand as he breathes, his tormentor oblivious to his internal battle as she manually checks over his body.

He knows what they'll do if they discover this secret—his one remaining link to a humanity neither he, nor they, wish to be reminded of. It will be like it was when they rid him of his body's reaction to pain: unrelenting stimulation until his receptors cease to respond.

He has endured months of agony. Months of sleep deprivation. Blood. Death.

But *touch...*

The warmth of human connection. The pleasure of another sentient being's caress.

His nerves hum under her fingertips as she stretches up to press against his face, testing newly healed flesh.

This is the one thing he has left that doesn't belong to them—and if they take this too, then he will truly be nothing but the machine they see him as.

That *she* sees him as.

He knows her name, but he tries not to use it, even in the quietude of his own mind. Thinking of his tormentor as a person makes it harder to slip into the nothingness that makes his time in her lab tolerable.

In the same way he is simply a sophisticated weapon to her, she is to him a nameless, faceless cog in the system that created him.

Except when she touches him.

In. Out.

"Still no pain?" she asks, stroking both hands down his shoulders with firm pressure, and he remembers how she answered a call in the lab a few weeks back. How the female voice on the other end called her Addie, the familiarity in the shortening of her name sparking his curiosity. To that woman, she is a person. Perhaps someone dear.

To him, she is anything but.

"No," he grinds out.

She flicks her gaze up to his, light gray eyes behind black-rimmed glasses taking in the tightness of his jaw. "Any tension? Discomfort?"

"No."

"Good." She steps around him to inspect his back, and her shoulder gently bumps against his arm as she does.

He isn't prepared for the pressure, isn't braced, and without thinking, he sucks in a small breath, tasting her scent.

A faint whiff of her floral shampoo fills his nostrils, and panic hits his brainstem. But it's too late; the kiss of her smell blooms on his palate, warm and female and *human,* and his body reacts.

Shit.

There is nothing he can do. They left too much man in him, too much alpha. His abdomen tenses, heat pooling low. Every touch of her fingertips against his back only tightens the pull in his groin, and it's maddening and revolting, and *fuck,* he never wants her to stop...

She does, of course. Once she is sure her prized soldier is fit for battle once more, she pulls her hands from his skin and steps around to his front again. And that? That is why human touch is the worst of the tortures he endures.

It feels like having found the narrowest ledge on an otherwise mirror-smooth cliff surface. Like being allowed one final breath of relief, of hope, before the ledge crumbles and he plummets into the depths of despair once more.

She makes a small noise of consternation, and when he dares a glance at her, her cheeks are tinged pink.

She moves her gaze from his hard member rising proudly between his thighs, but she doesn't meet his eyes when she says, "If you experience *urges*, AX2, you are instructed to take care of them. Privately."

"Yes, ma'am."

She flattens her lips to a line, and he braces for the sting of his chip. In the beginning, when he had yet to learn caution, she tried to dissuade his *urges* with pain. Eventually she conceded, but made it clear he is to handle his biological needs when alone in the lab at night.

But today, no punishment follows from the chip imbedded in his brain.

"All this technology at our fingertips, and I still can't separate the baseness of alpha biology without losing the strength you need to survive your conditioning," she says, the same irritation from before flaring in her voice. "It's been more than three *years* since your class was created, and we've been unable to make another successful proto-type since. But every soldier we mold after those same blueprints has *alpha issues*." She makes a gesture in the vague direction of his erection without looking directly at it. "Too much aggression, too much dominance, too much *need*."

There are others like him? He blinks, shock throbbing through his blood. She has never spoken to him about *others* before, nor blatantly shown annoyance at the flaws she finds in him.

It's the most human she has ever allowed herself to be in his presence.

She huffs out a breath and rubs a hand over her forehead, gaze flicking to his for a short moment. "Ensure you are at optimal functionality by tomorrow morning. We will be honored by a visit from the general at nine hundred hours, and he is bringing guests. He will expect nothing but perfection. Which means *I* expect nothing but perfection."

She gives him one final, hard look before she turns to leave the stasis chamber.

Through the thick glass to the lab, he sees her switching off the fluorescent fixtures, leaving only a faint glow from various bits of electronics to illuminate the room beyond. Seconds later, the sound of the door locking behind her lets AX2 know that he is alone.

Slowly he allows his muscles to soften, his stance becoming imperceptibly less rigid even as her words echo in his mind. Something stirs in his gut—something nearly as base, nearly as human, as the yearnings her scent ignited.

Others. There are *others*.

He is not alone.

TWO

ADDIE

"This is where you train them?"

The incredulity in General Thompson's voice makes me hide a grimace behind my tight smile. "Yes. All our data supports the need for as little stimulation during training and downtime as possible. It has proven the best way to manage any, ah, *temperament* issues."

He snorts and moves closer to the protective glass separating us from the white-painted, sparsely equipped training room where my oldest remaining cyborg stands, eyes locked on some point behind us.

"By boring the man out of his skull? Please. Forty-six years I've served, and never have I heard of a soldier who sharpened up by being locked in a sterile room twenty-four-seven."

"With respect, General, he is not a man; he is a lethal

weapon. They all are." I touch my fingertips to the data pad I'm clutching and flick the button activating AX2's chip. A shiver travels down the large soldier's body, imperceptible to the uninformed observer. "A simple scan of your biometrics and you can control him as perfectly as any missile. Would you care to demonstrate for our guests, sir?"

General Thompson exhales, an impatient sound, but the three CIA agents he has brought in to see AX2 shift closer. While their faces reveal nothing, it's not hard to decipher their interest. After all, what self-respecting intelligence agency wouldn't want to learn more about a lethal asset who can be controlled via a data pad?

The general takes the pad from me, his silent reprimand wiping the twitch of satisfaction off my lips. Right. He doesn't find my work worthy of pride, even if I'm one of the main scientists responsible for the strongest soldiers at the Pentagon's disposal.

I clasp my wrist in front of me and step back, schooling my expression as General Thompson scans his biometrics into my data pad.

"And now?"

"If you push the button for the microphone, you can give him whichever command you please," I instruct. "His chip is set to limited autonomy, so you don't have to be exact. He is trained to employ his best judgement in how to fulfil your orders, but he will be compelled to execute them."

"Compelled how, exactly?" one of the CIA agents asks while the general instructs AX2 to do some warm-up stretches.

"AX2 is fitted with a chip capable of overriding whatever impulses his brain would generate on its own. If given a direct order, he will obey. It is no different than programming a computer to launch missiles, or steering a tank.

"The chip has three settings: complete autonomy, limited autonomy, or full remote control. Currently, the AX class operates in limited autonomy mode during missions, but we have found that after about half a year, their training allows for safe activation of complete autonomy during most of their downtime hours."

I nod toward AX2 as the general commands him to begin the training course. He looks like a normal soldier in his fatigues and combat boots—or as normal as an alpha so hugely muscular can look. But when he grabs the rope dangling from the ceiling and leaps into the air to begin the course, it becomes evident he is anything but.

"How does he move so fast?" one of the visitors asks. Even her CIA training is unable to mask her incredulity. "That is... That should not be possible."

I follow AX2 with my gaze as he scales a twenty-foot

barrier in two leaps, then scrambles underneath the barbed wire in the blink of an eye. "It would be impossible, were he human. But he is not. He may look like a man, and if you were inclined to have a conversation with him, he may respond like one, but he is more a product of engineering than biology."

"What manner of missions has he completed thus far?" the leader of the little group asks. "Is he calibrated for more... delicate matters?"

I glance at the general. "Discussion of classified missions is above my paygrade, I'm afraid. But the AX class is highly trainable. I see no reason why any necessary skills should be unattainable."

"I will brief the deputy director on any details, should your agency decide to move forward with this... collaboration," General Thompson says. "For now, I believe Dr. Green is waiting to show you some of our newer AX recruits. They should provide a demonstration of how quickly they can be trained." He turns to the microphone again. "At ease, soldier."

AX2 comes to an immediate standstill, his eyes flicking over the windowpane separating him from us before he looks straight ahead.

I refrain from grimacing at the mention of Green and shake hands with our visitors as they offer polite thanks for the demonstration. They leave, clearly eager to see further examples of my work, despite their coldly professional expressions.

Yes, *my* work. Fuck Green.

"I want to talk with him."

I blink, surprised that the general is lingering here instead of following our visitors out. "With who? AX2?"

"Yes." Without waiting for my response, he approaches the heavy steel door separating us and types in the code.

"Why?" I blurt, but he's already moving through the now-open door with long strides, and I have to take two steps for every one of his to keep pace as he nears AX2.

General Thompson throws me a warning look over his shoulder. He doesn't verbalize the reprimand, but he doesn't need to.

I manage to stop myself from cowering as the instinct not to anger the alpha kick in, but I do correct myself. "Sorry, I meant: Why do you wish to speak with him, *sir?* We try to keep engagements to a minimum so as to not stimulate any unwanted responses. The AX model can be... challenging, if not kept firmly in check."

He sighs, as if I'm a child who shouldn't need to ask the obvious, and nods at AX2. "Because as much as you and the other doctors insist he is a machine, he was a man first. I've read the reports—what you call *challenges with their biochemical balance* looks to me like men in need of letting off some steam. Prisoners undergoing solitary confinement exhibit similar bursts of temper."

I clench my hands into fists behind him—a small

rebellion he'll never see. What I really want to do is scream.

"*Sir*. We base our conclusions on vigorous scientific research—"

The general silences me with a raised hand, his gaze locking with AX2's. He is nearly as tall as the cyborg, but I know he couldn't measure up to his muscular frame, even in his prime. No human can, alpha or not.

"Thank you for the demonstration, soldier," he says. "I'm curious—if you had the option, would you choose to spend your free time among other soldiers? Or do you prefer the solitude of Dr. Thompson's lab?"

"*Sir*," I hiss, outrage heating my cheeks. My knuckles are white with the effort of containing my anger. "Please. You'll undo months of traini—"

Once again, he silences me with a raised hand without sparing me so much as a glance. "AX2?"

The cyborg's green eyes flick to mine for the briefest second before he says, "I serve the U.S. government. My desires are unimportant."

"See?" I all but growl. "He does not need to *let off steam*, General. He is a *thing*—a weapon."

"Please," the general scoffs. "Torture any man for a few months, and he would respond similarly."

"Excuse me? I don't *torture*—!"

"So far, we have employed the AX2 models on relatively simple missions. It is the desire of the powers that be that we expand upon their usage for more complex tasks, some of which will require working closely with other soldiers—missions we can't employ *machines* for. For that, they will need to socialize. Relearn how to work as part of a team." The general arcs both eyebrows at AX2. "Do you remember, soldier? What it's like to be part of a unit?"

"No, sir," AX2 says, the rumbly bass of his voice not betraying any hint of interest.

Because he has none, I remind myself as I scour his blank expression. *He's incapable of emotion.*

But even as I think it, a flash of memory heats my cheeks and makes goosebumps crawl down my arms: the undeniable yearning in his eyes as his grotesque member swelled in response to my examination yesterday.

No. Not emotion. Instinct—basic biology. Even insects possess the drive to procreate. And I have yet to figure out how to strip that impulse from the AX class.

Green doesn't see the need, but then I doubt he's had to endure their leftover *alpha urges* while trying to get on with work.

"If you recall, we don't know if AX2 has been part of a unit before," I say, the embarrassing memory from yesterday stripping my ability to keep my voice sufficiently respectful. I'm done caring.

General Thompson arcs one eyebrow a millimeter higher at my insolent tone, but finally deigns to look at me.

"He was a soldier long before you came across him, my dear. He's got that look about him."

I bare my teeth at the inappropriate moniker, the heat in my cheeks deepening. "Either way, he doesn't need to be *socialized* to be capable of more complex missions. Tell me what you need him to do and I'll make sure he's ready. I don't need your help to do my job."

He sighs and pats my shoulder. "I know you're a brilliant scientist, Addie, but some things you can't learn from a book. What I need is for him and the others to be ready for full social integration so they can complete any mission the Agency requires. The Russians are becoming increasingly, ah, *problematic*. The AX class could prove an invaluable asset—they are miles ahead of any technology our enemy has on their hands, so far as intelligence can discern. But we need them to be more than machines. *You* need to make them into more than that. Understood?"

And if the AX class happens to be the solution to this Russian problem, he as the general in charge of this project will be lauded. There are only so many opportunities left for a three-star general to climb in the ranks, but I suspect he has ambitions for the next step. He always has.

"Understood. *Sir*," I bite out.

The general shakes his head, but doesn't reprimand me. My father is many things, but he is not a hypocrite.

He nods at AX2 and crosses the floor to the exit. Before he leaves, he turns to say, "Your mother wants you to come by for dinner tonight. Can I tell her you'll be there?"

"I will." I dig my nails into my palms as the door swings shut behind him. It's not his fault. He's an alpha—he's never known what it is to have to fight for respect. To know that any glimpse of softness will ruin everything you've worked for.

I glance at AX2, who is still standing perfectly still, gaze trained on a spot on the far wall. There is not so much as a flicker in his expression to suggest he's noted the unprofessional exchange between the general and myself.

But then, there shouldn't be. He knows better than most that I have no softness to be exploited.

THREE
AX2

There are five AX models in existence.

AX2 stares at the four men-that-aren't in the training room.

The ever-present stench of bleach doesn't hide the cocktail of alpha scent in the air, but even without it, he'd know what they are—or at least what the biological part of them is. They are all wide with muscle, and there's a sharpness in their eyes as they watch one another, reading every movement to determine whether they are surrounded by enemies or allies. *Alphas*.

He suspects that if any of them had been given a choice, they would have opted to socialize with betas and women. He feels it too—the biological urge to assert his dominance over four powerful rivals—but *fuck*, it doesn't matter. They're here, he's not alone, and the space in his gut he thought held nothing but despair is now tight with a tingling *awareness* that reaches all the way around to his tailbone.

Without a word, he crosses the floor to the nearest alpha—a young man with short, white-blond hair and ice-blue eyes first widening in surprise at his approach, then narrowing as he doesn't stop. AX2 ignores the unspoken threat and reaches out, grabs the man by the shoulder, and pulls him to his chest with enough force to send a shock-wave through him at the impact.

A growl escapes the other alpha at the uninvited touch, but quiets to a huff of surprised laughter when AX2 wraps both arms around him and hugs him tight.

Touch.

He's touching another living, breathing being. Someone like him.

He's not alone, after all.

Something he didn't know still existed clicks into place in his brain, but he is too numb to do more than grunt as the sensation of humanity slowly filters through his consciousness.

Too late, he remembers why he can't let *them* see this —the white-clad doctors no doubt observing them like the lab-rats they are—what will happen if *she* learns of the weakness he has kept hidden for so long. Swallowing a curse, he releases his hold on the other alpha, but before he can step back, the blond man mutters, "Oh, fuck it," and wraps his own arms around AX2.

A bouquet of sensation slams through him: warmth, comfort, and relief drown out his momentary anger at another alpha constricting him. The fear of what *she* will do to him at this display of weakness lingers, but he can't find the willpower to break away. For this one moment, he'll take whatever punishment she inflicts to erase his remaining shred of humanity.

Kinship. The word echoes in his mind, trickling through his veins and into his organs still made of flesh. Expanding until it hurts. These strangers are his kin; he is not alone.

Warm, solid muscle presses against his back as the others join them one by one. No one speaks for several long moments. The only sound is the slow, deep breathing of five sets of lungs, artificial and not.

"I'd still trade every single one of you for half an hour with a whore," someone mutters from behind him, finally breaking the peaceful silence.

The young blond who has his arms around AX2 lets out a laugh. It rings in his ears and pierces his brain, alien in its genuineness.

"Half an hour? It'd take you twenty-eight minutes to find the hole? Shit, how long's it been that you'd forget *that?* I haven't been thinking about much else for the past six months."

A guffaw. "See how much *you* remember after nearly two years, you little twat."

AX2 remembers this—the jokes, the laughter, the sharing of words for no other reason than... than *bonding*. It's like a lightning strike up his spine, only it isn't a memory as such, it's... it's a whisper through the dark parts of his mind he can no longer access. A warm trickle through his blood. It feels... right in a way nothing else has since the cursed day he woke up in *her* lab.

This? This is what it feels like to be human.

A clank of metal sends a jerk through the group, each alpha pulling away and into straight-spined postures of attention before the door swings open.

AX2's heart throbs too fast in his chest as General Thompson walks in, followed by Dr. Green, and a few moments later, *her*. The general's gaze slides over them all, and with a jolt of surprise, AX2 realizes the fear making his heart pound against his ribs is not for himself—it's for the strangers he's known for mere minutes.

He moves forward a single step, offering a mechanical salute. "General, I initiated any and all unapproved contact. The responsibility for any infractions is mine, and mine alone."

The blond alpha by his side draws in a sharp breath, imperceptible to a regular human's ears, but AX2 hears it. The gratitude he feels at that small suggestion that this stranger cares what consequences he might face for his admission is blinding. But the urge to shield these men from whatever punishment comes next is impossible to dismiss. They are his kin.

And he is not alone.

But instead of anger or disapproval, the general's face cracks in a wide grin.

"Ha! Do you see this?" He turns to look over his shoulder at the two doctors. "Five minutes together, and they are already displaying unit loyalty. *Machines.*" His focus returns to AX2, the triumphant smile still in place. "Step back, soldier. No infractions have taken place."

This... is new. AX2 obeys, unease clenching in his gut as he flicks his gaze to *her*. *New* is dangerous with her. And judging by the murderous look in her pale gray eyes, she does not agree with the general's assessment. Her *father's* assessment.

It is... odd to think of her as having a father. Unpleasant. *Addie,* he'd called her. The same, shortened name the woman on the phone had used for her. The doctor hadn't liked it, hadn't liked being undermined in front of him, the look of anger on her face as prominent then as it is now.

"You may be wondering why we have gathered you together," General Thompson says, his focus widening to include the other soldiers. "Through the hard work of the scientists working on Project Fireshield, the U.S. Military now has five soldiers amongst its ranks with unprecedented strength. You have all been tested through a series of complex missions, and we are most impressed with your combat abilities. Your unique qualities have ensured success where drones would have lacked finesse, and regular troops strength. Your victories have not gone unnoticed. The Pentagon has tasked me with taking your training in a new direction, and that, men, is why we are here today.

"For the past four decades, I have served our country, and the number-one lesson I have learned is that a man needs his unit. It doesn't matter how strong you are, soldiers.; without brothers in arms, you are vulnerable. Weak. It is my wish, and the wish of the U.S. Government, that you integrate into the general military population. The eventual goal is that you form a special unit that can assist every branch of the defensive services as needed.

"Your combat prowess is impeccable, so going forward, you'll be developing skills of a more social nature. Step one is to bring you together, like we have today, and to assess how you might operate as a unit. I have already provided Dr. Green and Dr. Thompson with your new regimen, and they will be overseeing your progress and reporting back to me.

"I have great expectations of you, men. Each of you has already shown how seriously you take this second chance you have been given to serve your country, and I expect nothing less as we move forward together. Now, I have duties to return to, so I will leave you with your capable team to get on with it. Good luck, soldiers. Do me proud."

No one speaks as General Thompson nods at the two doctors, then turns to exit the room.

A vein throbs in AX2's temple, one of his body parts untouched by engineering. He saw the people with the general yesterday: sleek suits and bland faces with cunning eyes. The kind of people at home in the shadows. *Intelligence.*

It doesn't take a genius to work out why they were watching a demonstration of his abilities, not when it is immediately followed by orders to learn to *socialize.*

He dares a glance at *her* again, at her flatly pressed lips and darkened eyes, and remembers how she all but snarled that she could get him to follow any instructions necessary.

The thought has barely entered his brain when she lifts her gaze, catching his.

Addie.

Her much-too-sweet name flickers through his mind before he can stop it, followed by the memory of her floral shampoo in his nostrils. Her fingertips on his chest. In the breath their eyes are locked, something dark and needy coils in his abdomen. Then her eyes widen, outrage flashing over her face before she rips her gaze from him and turns to the other soldiers.

"You know your orders: socialize. We will be observing your efforts. Noncompliance will not be accepted. Commence."

"Speaking of whores," the man to his left mutters under his breath, low enough that neither doctor hears.

AX2 blinks, the rushing sound in his ears making it hard to focus on the other soldiers hesitantly relaxing. The knot in his abdomen is still hot and tight, and he feels... empty. *Hungering.*

What is this?

"AX2." Dr. Green snaps his fingers. "Join the others."

He jerks once, finally managing to pull his focus from the disturbing sensations of his biological body. "Yes, sir."

The others watch him, faces blank from what he assumes is the same sort of training that has taught him to keep his emotions hidden. But when he joins the loose circle of men, a dark-haired alpha with olive skin asks, "AX2?"

AX2 grunts, offering a nod. "You?"

"AX6." He reaches out a hand. The movement is a little stilted, like he's forgotten how to move his muscles for the gesture. "Dwayne."

AX2 blinks, hesitating a long second before he puts his palm to AX6's—*Dwayne's.* It's warm and dry, and the sensation blinds him for a heartbeat.

The others mirror them, murmuring introductions.

The young, blond alpha he hugged is AX23. He calls himself Jack.

AX2 blinks as every man offers a name to go along with his serial number. AX9 is Sean. AX21 is Simon.

"Shit, they must have lost a lot of us, eh?" Sean, the man who called *her* a whore, says, shaking his head once as he looks them all over. His eyes land on AX2. "I didn't catch your name, bud."

His name. The concept seems so ludicrous—the mere thought that *she* would grant him humanity in the form of a name is enough to make him scoff. "The only designation I've been given is AX2."

"No, I mean—your name. You have to have had one before, right?" Sean insists, furrowing his auburn brows.

Before? AX2 opens his mouth, but no words come out. They... They remember what was before?

"They took your memories?" Dwayne murmurs, his voice too quiet to project back to where the doctors stand with clipboards, observing them. "Dr. Green once mentioned... He said I was the first to retain 'em. Something about not being able to keep us stable without them. But you're okay?"

Okay. Something bubbles AX2's his gut—a wild urge to laugh, perhaps. Or cry; he can't tell which.

In the end, he does neither. "I'm alive."

"I guess that's better than it could have been," Simon

says. "I'd have died without this... procedure. Shot in action. I assume it's the same for the rest of you?"

Murmurs of agreement. AX2 stays silent. He was told he was dying—beyond medical help. That this was the only thing that could have saved his life.

That he should be grateful.

Yet since the day he awoke in this cursed place, *gratitude* has been the furthest thing from his mind.

Unbidden, his gaze slips back to *her*. In those first, confused moments after waking, he'd thought her an angel, her pale face outlined by the fluorescent lights of her lab, her voice soft and pulling on the very fabric of his being.

He'd soon learned the truth.

Hatred churns in his gut as he stares at her, the voices of the others fading to a murmur. They are exchanging stories of their deaths, of their memories from before. But she took his. Even now, among peers he didn't know he had, but has yearned for for so long, she has ensured he's alone.

The urge to close his hands around her throat makes his fingers twitch. He can almost feel her warm skin under his palms, the frantic jump of her pulse. See her eyes widen and naked fear take the place of haughty disdain. He has killed before—every mission has resulted in the loss of at least one life. None of them gave him any satisfaction, but *her*... Just the thought of her fragile little neck in his grasp heats his body and makes his skin prickle with pleasure.

As if she senses the intensity in his stare, she looks up from her notes, once more catching his eyes. Anger flares in hers at his second transgression within mere minutes, her knuckles whitening around her clipboard. She parts her lips, and he braces for the pain of his chip responding to whatever order she's about to bark at him—but instead she hisses something he can't hear to the other scientist.

Dr. Green looks up, focus narrowing in on AX2 before his mouth hikes up in a lopsided grin. "It's to be expected, Thompson. Their biological side will be running rampant after being deprived for so long. Maybe it's best if you skip out, hmm?"

Bright pink splotches color her cheeks, and this time AX2 hears her clearly: "This is *my* project, Green. I am not about to abandon it because of this... folly!"

Dr. Green shrugs and returns his focus to his own clipboard. "Suit yourself. But if the others get the same idea, there's a good chance this little bonding exercise will turn into a bid for dominance. And if you ruin the Pentagon's plans for the AX class, I don't think you'll get the chance to so much as cry 'sexism' before your ass is permanently booted off the project."

She doesn't respond, and for the longest moment she just stands there, fingers clenched so tight around her clipboard the stiff plastic bows under the pressure. Then she turns her head and stares again at AX2, and the sheer amount of *hatred* in her eyes makes his own flicker away.

When she spins on her heel and stomps out of the room, he can still feel the sear of that hatred, a warm spike all the way down his spine and into his pelvis.

FOUR
ADDIE

I spend three hours pacing the silent halls of the compound, where I have resided for most of my waking hours since finishing my doctorate.

When I arrived here, they had been working on fusing flesh with technology for years without having ever produced a viable soldier.

Thirty-one months after I entered the building, AX1 opened his eyes. On *my* table. The AX class is *mine*.

And yet... I know Dr. Green is right. The Pentagon will kick me off the project without hesitation if they so much as suspect I'll be a *distraction* to the alpha nature I have tried, and failed, to extract for precisely this reason.

Disgusting, degrading, *base* bastards! Three *years* I have trained AX2 to complete obedience, three-goddamn-*years* of programming his mind to focus on nothing but the next mission, and all of it is undone within twenty minutes of my father's harebrained scheme.

An unbidden shudder travels through me as an image of AX2's green eyes flash through my memory: *Want.*

Mere minutes after being allowed to access his primitive side, and his alpha brain flicks to sex. It doesn't matter that I'm his superior, that I fucking *created* him, because deep down he's still just a beast, and to him—to every single one of them—I will never be more than *female.* Nothing but a hole to knot.

I clench my fists until the sting of my nails boring into my palms makes the memory of that dark hunger in AX2's eyes wither away. I will be damned if I let anyone displace me from my own project. And it will be a cold day in hell before I allow AX2 to so much as *think* about dominating me in any way, shape, or form.

***

THE LAB CONTAINING AX2's stasis chamber lies in shadows, only one overhead light illuminating the sprawling room. I pause when I see movement through the large window displaying the inside of my workplace. No one comes down here, apart from the cleaning crew, and I am diligent to only ever schedule them for when AX2 is out on a mission. I am the only one who enters this lab, except for five days a month when Dr. Green has to fill in *for my own safety*.

I bite the inside of my cheek until I taste blood.

Another flash of movement draws my attention, and I frown. AX2 paces between equipment and computers, his skin rippling over bulging muscles as he flexes his hands and rolls his head and shoulders. Normally he spends his waking hours within the confines of the stasis chamber, staring silently ahead hours on end. Orders to never touch any of the expensive equipment are embedded in his chip, but they have never been necessary.

Now, though—now the looks he throws at my main computer and the device I use to measure the flow of electricity between his brain and artificial body parts makes me think I'd have lost a few hundred thousand dollars' worth of equipment without it.

Undoubtedly another side-effect of Dad's insistence that we allow *socialization*.

Gritting my teeth, I swipe my access card over the small screen next to the door and push through the opening the second a green light flashes.

AX2 freezes at the sound of the door slamming shut behind me, the dilation of his pupils as he takes me in the only movement of his suddenly still body.

"You are agitated," I say. An observation, not a question. "You will calm yourself. Immediately."

He doesn't respond, but his jaw ticks.

I narrow my eyes. It has been a very, very long time since AX2 has fought me in even the smallest of ways. "Do you need a reminder of who is in charge, AX2?"

There's a long beat of silence as we stare each other down. Then, finally: "No, ma'am."

His voice is a deep rumble, the anger in it nearly imperceptible. Nearly.

"Is there something you wish to get off your chest, soldier?" I arc my eyebrow, daring him to speak.

"Why did you take my memories?"

The question comes so immediately, it takes me by surprise. I blink once before I catch myself.

"The others—you let them keep theirs. Why did you take mine?" he presses, green eyes darkening further. *Hatred.* There is pure, unadulterated hatred in them, and it makes my heart pick up speed.

My body's involuntary reaction to the unspoken threat of his strength only infuriates me further. But I am not a mere animal; I am better than that, better than *him.*

I retain my composure. The lie rolls smoothly off my tongue: "The condition you were found in, the circumstances... memories would not have been a boon for you. As it turns out, it has allowed you to focus on your missions far better than the rest of your class. Unfortunately, the survival rate was too low for the soldiers who followed you, so we had to adjust our methods."

His eyes are still dark, the tension in his shoulders and

bared chest speaking of the anger he is holding back. I set my jaw against the tremor in my gut—I may be cursed with the same instincts to surrender as every other woman or beta faced with a furious alpha, but I would rather die than submit.

Not that I will ever have to again, because here, in *my* lab, I'm the one in control.

"Kneel."

He stares at me for a long second, this big, muscled brute. I know his stats by heart—he is 6'11" and 411 pounds of pure power, and of the many, many men he has killed in the past three years, 36 of them have been with his bare hands. He dwarfs me in every way. Every way... but one.

I give him a small smile as he lowers himself first on one knee, then the other, surrendering all that strength to me because I am the one with the real power.

I could have forced him to his knees with the chip— just one word, and his body is mine to command—but I don't have to. Not anymore.

Even with my father's idiotic interference, even after he's been reminded of the biology that I have spent so long taming to obedience, AX2 still submits to my commands simply because I will it.

I walk toward him, every step controlled to show him how little impact his anger has on me, and stop right in front of his kneeling figure.

He stares blindly at my midsection, unmoving. His breathing is steady and silent. Uncowed.

Anger fizzes in my gut. I reach out without thought, wrapping my fingers around his chin to force his face up. The warmth of his skin is a shock to my system, but I temper the urge to recoil, gripping tighter instead. "Look at me."

His green eyes flick up to meet mine, anger still darkening their depths.

"I want you to remember what your time with me was like when you first came here," I say, my voice a soft counterpoint to the iron grip I keep on his ruggedly handsome face. It is impossible to tell where artificial skin meets biological. *I* did that. "How many months of pain you endured while you became the formidable weapon you are today. Do you remember, AX2?"

"I remember, ma'am."

I smile thinly. "Good. Because I do understand how... *confusing* this new approach must be for you. You have spent years shedding your, ah, social impulses, and then here we are, suddenly *encouraging* them.

"But I want you to remember those first long, difficult months you endured, and I want you to never, ever forget. Because if you *ever* again look at me like I'm something you can fuck, I will *hurt* you like you've never imagined possible. Do you understand?"

For the first time since I entered the lab, the anger in

AX2's gaze sways. Not out of fear, nor respect—instead there's a flicker of confusion. Blankness sweeps it away. "Ma'am. I have no such desires."

He dares *lie* to me? I grit my teeth and slip my hand from his chin to his throat, squeezing. His pulse thrums under my fingers, only slightly elevated, the muscles in his neck too thick for me to be able to do any damage, even if I tried. But all I want is the reminder that I can take away his life far more easily than I gave it.

"No? Then tell me, *soldier*: What went through your mind when you were staring at me in that room? This is a command, AX2."

He draws in a sharp breath, unhindered by my fingers against his windpipe, his eyes widening ever-so slightly. It's all the warning I get before he's on his feet, knocking my arm away with the movement, and wrapping his massive hand around my throat.

I squeak, an undignified noise. It's the only sound I manage before he squeezes, and my ability to speak dies on a rattle. The next second, he shoves me backwards by his grip on my throat and slams me against the window to the stasis chamber so hard pain bursts through my muscles.

What is happening? Disbelief fades for terror as I stare up at the enormous alpha soldier who has me pinned at arm's length. He's not supposed to be able to do this! He can't hurt me, I made sure—

His face is still blank, the only sign of emotion that darkness in his haunting eyes, and belatedly I realize that, yes... he *can* hurt me—as long as his desire to do so outweighs the debilitating pain from his chip. I can see it in his eyes, that terrible agony searing his nervous system as he disregards one of the first, most fundamental orders I gave him. He is in far more pain than any man should be capable of bearing, yet it is nothing compared to the blazing hatred in his gaze as he stares me down.

"I thought about killing you," he says softly, his gaze flicking from mine down to where his hand is wrapped tight around my throat, making it hard to breathe and impossible to say the words that would resume my control over him. And save my life.

Naked terror pounds in my veins as I wheeze for breath, survival instincts finally kicking into gear at his words. I claw at his arm, my nails drawing superficial lines of red on his skin and revealing the gleaming metal beneath.

This can't be happening! I can't die—not like this. Please, not like this.

AX2 watches my pathetic fight for survival impassively, unmoved by my scratching and kicking, his hand warm and unyielding around my throat. Just one little twitch of those inhuman muscles and he'll break my neck. One flinch and I'll die at the hand of my own creation.

I whimper at the yawning realization of my own

imminent death, the sound gargled and raw. It draws his attention back up from my neck to my eyes, a soft sound leaving his full lips. *Surprise.*

He reaches forward with his free hand, touching my cheek. When he retrieves his fingers, wetness glistens on their tips.

A small frown pulls his dark brows in as he stares at my anguished tears on his digits as if their presence there is perplexing. An unsolvable mystery.

And then he touches them to his mouth. Tasting my fear.

Another noise leaves his lips, rougher than before, the sound traveling up from the depths of his chest, his eyelids fluttering shut.

"You taste—" He cuts himself off, exhaling shakily. Then slowly he opens his eyes again.

Hunger.

It's not outrage that grips me by the gut in the face of the alpha's carnal attention this time.

I scream brokenly against his crushing hold on my neck, clawing and kicking and frantic as the giant beast closes the distance between our bodies, bends his head to my neck, and sniffs me.

He grunts, the sound deep and rich, the exhale of his breath tickling right below my ear, the warmth of his body overwhelming. And... and something low in my abdomen seems to... *melt.*

I stiffen, my futile attempts at freeing myself stilling entirely. What... What is this?

AX2 grunts again, his breath raising goosebumps along my neck. His grip on my throat eases the tiniest bit, allowing me to suck in a deeper breath, and I get a lungful of his scent.

It's one of the things I haven't been able to strip from his biological half: his alpha scent. But it's never smelled like *this* before. This... *warm*.

His nose brushes against the tendon in my neck, a small gasp leaving his lungs as he breathes me in, and that *something* low in my abdomen... *softens*.

Readying me.

The thought flashes through my brain the same moment he lifts his head up from my neck and flicks his gaze back to mine.

No, no, no, no! This can't be happening—*this isn't happening!* I strike without thought of anything but the need for this nightmare to end, but he's close enough for me to finally make impact, and I hit him square in one prominent cheekbone.

Pain explodes through my knuckles, and my vision blurs with a fresh bout of tears.

AX2 grunts, a surprised sound. When I blink my vision clear, he is staring at me with wide eyes slowly filling with horror. Horror that soon morphs into utter disgust.

Baring his teeth, he swings around and shoves me away from him, making me stumble until I collide with a chair and fall smack on my ass on the concrete floor. My tailbone smarts, and AX2 hisses and presses the hand no longer around my throat to the side of his head, undoubtedly in response to his chip's punishment for hurting me. It's the first reaction he's shown since he snatched me by the throat.

"Abort autonomy," I wheeze, my throat struggling to expand around my voice. "Abort, abort, abort!"

AX2 drops his hand from his head, his body resetting to attention and his face smoothing to the blank mask of nothing. *Safe.*

Shakily, I force several deep breaths into my lungs. *You're okay. He can't hurt you now.*

Fury ignites deep in my chest and rises like a serpent. He... He thought he could...

He *grabbed* me!

I stagger to my feet and bare my teeth at the giant beast. *"Kneel."*

This time he drops to his knees immediately, his body obeying my command without the delay of free will. He rests his knuckles lightly against the concrete floor and looks up at me impassively, awaiting my next order. There is no more anger in his eyes. No more of anything.

I growl with mounting rage. He thinks he gets to

escape into mindless oblivion? After what he did to me? No. No, absolutely not!

"Engage pain receptors," I spit.

A fine tremor works its way through his strong body. I stare at his face, waiting. Three minutes pass before he begins to breathe heavier, his sides flexing with the expansion of his lungs. Five more, and a light sheen of sweat covers his skin.

Twenty-some minutes later, I finally see the flash of awareness in his eyes, and I smirk with triumph. *Can't hide from me, soldier.*

"Disengage pain receptors."

The only outward sign of the lack of stimulus to his nervous system is a slight easing of his muscles. His breath still comes hard and fast, his skin glistening with perspiration—but his eyes are bright with consciousness as he returns my stare. I see the hatred in them plain as day.

"There you are," I whisper. I try to say something more—to tell him he can hate me for as long as he can hold out—but my voice dies on a raspy exhale before a single word escapes.

Heat floods my body, languid and deep, making me aware of every hair standing on end across my body. The sensation of the laboratory air against my skin feels... somehow *more* than normal. *Feels too much.*

I stare unblinkingly at the kneeling alpha—at his flexing muscles around his still-rapid breaths, his broad jaw, at the sheer *power* of him. Without my permission, a tremor spreads from my still-bruised tailbone, up my spine and down my arms.

I open my mouth again, but no sound escapes.

His eyes are mesmerizing.

The thought is fleeting and comes unbidden. I sway unsteadily on my feet, pulled by some invisible magnetism in those green depths. I've never known a man with eyes like that—

But he's not a man.

I force my mind to still. *What is this? Never* have I had to remind myself of AX2's true nature, no matter how much he looks like a man. I've hardwired the technology within him myself, grown the cells of his artificial skin in my own lab. I *know* what he is, and man it is not. But why... Why is my mind so foggy? Why can't I look away from the smoldering hatred in those haunting eyes?

My breathing is as fast as his, panic clawing at the edges of the fog swathing my brain. Something's wrong with me. Something's terribly, irrevocably *wrong,* but all I can do is stare at the kneeling alpha while my body shakes like a leaf.

Is it delayed shock? A panic attack? A freaking seizure? I need help. I need to find someone who can help me!

At that last thought, my body finally moves. But

instead of running for the exit, I stumble forward. Toward *him*.

I only make it three steps before the heat in my body rushes south into my abdomen, and *something* low inside me tightens so instantaneously, I nearly lose my footing.

"*Oooh!*" My cry starts sharp, but turns to a soft croon by the end as the tightness below my navel becomes molten and my sex... *softens*.

I stop abruptly, naked realization finally making it through the haze as I stare in mounting horror into AX2's eyes. No. This isn't possible. He's a fucking *machine!*

But my body doesn't care. Heat thrums through my veins, hardening my nipples and erasing everything that elevates me above base biology.

Heat.

With the last vestiges of my willpower, I stagger away from the kneeling alpha and out the door. And I flee.

Dr. Green finds him still kneeling on the concrete some long hours later. Morning, AX2 surmises, from the coffee-scented Styrofoam cup in the beta's hand.

Dr. Green stops in his tracks when he spots the alpha on the floor, his eyebrows high on his forehead. "Don't tell me Adelaide is playing hooky because of some sex game gone wrong."

Sex. The word pounds through his brain, shadowy talons raking his marrow. If he could, he'd shudder in response. He has gotten used to his body responding on someone else's command, but last night... Last night was *different.* And nothing like the times his flesh has reacted against his will to the gentle touch of her examinations, or the smell of her shampoo.

He could have killed her.

It would have killed him too, and what sweet relief that would have been. Yet when his fingers constricted around her throat, his body refused to complete the command. His body. Not his brain.

Not the chip.

The betrayal is still hot at the back of his throat. He had a chance to finally be free of this nightmare, free of *her*. And he didn't take it.

"AX2? Did Dr. Thompson get you to sleep with her last night?" Dr. Green asks.

"No, sir." The words come out monotone, the chip ensuring immediate compliance.

The beta eyes him as he takes a sip of his cup. "Did she try to?"

"No, sir."

"Hmm." Dr Green tilts his head, the corner of his mouth quirking up a couple of millimeters. "Did you *want* to fuck her?"

"Yes, sir." And there it is, the truth still making his insides tight with horror. Her throat under his fingers, the taste of her tears on his tongue, and the *smell* of her... His body had *yearned* for her, and not because he was starved for touch and so lonely he couldn't bear it. No. It'd been something far more primal, far more... intimate.

The beta male huffs a small laugh before he sips another mouthful of coffee. "Guess the general is right about you lot being more men than machines. Lock an alpha up for long enough, and he'll fuck anything with tits, eh? All right, let's get you sorted out, AX2. Dr. Thompson called in sick, so you're with me for the day. Engage autonomy mode."

AX2's muscles relax out of his artificially controlled posture the instant the chip releases its hold. Slowly, stretching organic flesh stiff from the many hours forced to hold still, he gets to his feet.

"Grab a shower. Jerk off, if you need to. Then get into some fresh trousers and come back to me," Dr. Green says, setting the Styrofoam cup down next to a computer as he begins clacking away at the attached keyboard. "No need for a shirt; I'll just have to remove it again for the electrodes. We're gonna run some tests, see if your wiring's still in balance after the socializing yesterday. And if I were you, I'd cross everything that it is. Seems you're way overdue for what the general's got planned next."

IT'S three days before AX2 learns what those plans are. Three days without *her*—the most she's ever been absent, outside of her five scheduled days every month—and no missions to offer his mind anything else to focus on.

He never thought he'd wish for those cursed assignments, but in between solitary meals and his five hours of daily exercise, there is nothing for him to do but think. And all his brain seems capable of focusing on is *her*.

When will she return to hurt him for what he did? Why didn't she complete his punishment that night? He knows all too well that she is capable of far more torment than she inflicted on him then. *Why did she run?*

Dr. Green comes to collect him an hour after breakfast, and he assumes he is to perform his daily exercises until they turn left at the branch of corridors leading away from where his training room is located.

The beta takes him to the same room where he met the others of the AX class earlier in the week. His pulse picks up speed as the doctor swipes his access card.

The others.

He hasn't thought much about them these past days. Every time he tries to recall the relief of knowing he isn't alone, his memories take him straight back to what happened later that night. To *her*.

The door swings open, and Dr. Green ushers him inside.

Three other AX soldiers are already there—Jack, Dwayne, and Simon. They are standing at attention at a pile of blankets each, faces blank. But when he catches Jack's crystal-blue eyes, the alpha gives him a faint smile.

Warmth spreads in AX2's chest, an unexpected bloom of something close to happiness. *His kin.*

"That's your nest," Dr. Green says, gesturing to a

heap of blankets at the far corner. "Go wait while I fetch AX9. I'll give you instructions when you're all here."

AX2 does as ordered, the door slamming shut behind the doctor's back before he reaches the blankets. He glances down at them. There are several, all neatly folded and in the same shade of gray, along with a few pillows. The fabric looks scratchy.

"Nest?" he asks no one in particular.

"You know, the bed-thing some girls make when they get broody," Dwayne says, a smile in his voice. "Don't tell me they took *those* memories from you too."

"My money's on horny lady cyborgs in heat," Simon says. "And we're the only ones who can sate them."

"Jesus Christ, you really have been here too long," Jack laughs. The sound is a warm rumble. "I bet it's just some form of team-building activity. And if you don't get rid of that hard-on, Lady Doc's gonna zap your balls the moment she steps foot in here."

AX2 looks up in time to see Simon grimace and reach into his pants to adjust himself.

"Swear to god, whatever it is, it better involve whores," Dwayne mutters. "One afternoon with human contact, and I've been fucking dying for a woman."

No one gets to respond. The door swings open, revealing Dr. Green and Sean. AX2's eyes light up at the sight of them.

"All right, go stand by the free nest, AX9," Dr Green

says with a nod in the direction of the remaining pile of blankets. When the alpha obeys him, he gives them a small smile. "Following the preliminary stages of your new training, there have been... a few incidents, shall we say. Occurrences which have made it clear that we need to alter the stimulus we provide in order to engage of your more human traits."

AX2 glances to his side, catching Dwayne's eyes. The doctors rarely bother explaining their procedures, let alone their reasons. This is *new*.

Tension coils in his back.

"General Thompson feels the best way to help you adjust to the tasks ahead is to provide you with an, ah, *outlet*. This morning, you will each be granted two hours with a companion." Green's smile slips off his face, his expression turning stern. "You are not allowed to discuss anything related to your abilities, your past missions, or the location of these premises. Do not do anything that will make me regret agreeing to this arrangement. That is a command."

The chip zings the tissue of AX2's brain, encoding the order. He blinks, still not quite sure he's heard the doctor right.

"Any questions before we proceed?"

"Companions, sir?" Dwayne croaks. The urgency in his voice resonates in AX2's gut. *Loneliness.* "Are they... women?"

The beta nods, his lips quirking up in another small smile. "Yes, AX6. They are female."

Simon chokes out a half-strangled sound. No one else says a word, but the tension in the room suddenly feels like a physical entity.

"If that is all... I will be back momentarily." Dr. Green says, raising both eyebrows as he looks over the five of them. "And remember—best behavior, hmm?"

There is only silence as they wait. No one moves. No one speaks. The bitter scent of aggression tinges the air, alpha pheromones thick in AX2's nostrils.

He breathes slowly, evenly, instincts keeping him still so as to not trigger a fight. These men with him, they may be his newly discovered kin, but this? This is a harsh test for their freshly forged loyalties. If it comes to a fight for these *companions*, it will be bloody.

Females. Outside of missions, he remembers only one such creature.

A shiver travels up his spine, and he grits his teeth against the image of *her* that flickers through his mind. Her panting breath. The drum of her pulse beneath his fingers...

The metallic clang of the door opening breaks through his spiraling thoughts, and he looks up in time to see Dr. Green step through, followed by five strangers.

One of the other soldiers inhales sharply. Sean tightens his hands into fists by his side.

They are clad in colorful fabrics that leave much of their skin exposed—tanned, pale, dark. They are a smorgasbord of femininity—overspilling cleavages, lushly rounded hips, softly curved arms. And the *smell* of them... Sweet perfumes intermingling over a warm, primal scent AX2's body recognizes as *woman* before his mind catches up. It cloys at his nostrils and lingers at the back of his throat, overriding the increasing stench of alpha aggression.

One of them giggles, the pearling sound entirely alien. "Ooh, they didn't say anything about how handsome you'd be! Aren't we lucky, girls?"

The others join in, filling the room with noises and smells his brain struggles to process as they spill in.

Dwayne, apparently much faster to work through the onslaught of new impressions, steps forward and grabs the nearest girl by the wrist.

"Oh!" She startles at the touch, then breaks into another giggle when he pulls her back to his pile of blankets, slips his arms around her soft body, and proceeds to bury his nose in her hair. "My, they weren't kidding when they said you'd been without women for a while, huh? Don't you worry, soldier. I'll take excellent care of you. Oh, that *tickles!*"

Awakened by Dwayne's conquest, the others move forward, snatching laughing women by the waists and hands and pulling them back to their corners. It is all so... easy. *Warm.*

New.

AX2 remains frozen by his blankets, his muscles tight around the sense of dread mounting in his chest. He should want this. He knows he should—but their scents overwhelm his senses, the colors of their clothes too bright when all he knows is searing white slashed with gray and darkness. Their voices ring too... *loud.* Too cheerful.

One girl remains alone, hovering by Dr. Green's side. She clasps her wrist with one hand and darts her gaze around the room, finally zeroing in on him. Her smile is immediate and wide. She casts a quick glance at the beta by her side, and encouraged by his nod, crosses the floor until she stops in front of AX2.

"Hi," she says, her long lashes lowering in mock shyness, even as her eyes rake over him with enough heat to prickle his skin. "I'm Candi."

She's got pretty dark eyes and painted lips, and black hair that shines like silk in the fluorescent light. A wide leather collar decorates her slim neck.

When he doesn't reply, the corners of her mouth quirk higher, and without being invited, she places both hands on his T-shirt-clad chest. "Shy, huh? That's okay. We can take it slow."

The shock of her touch rocks through him, a blaze of heat, even though she doesn't touch his skin. She smells like vanilla and *female,* but as she skims her small hands over his chest, his brain conjures up the uninvited memory of angry gray eyes.

Shit. He grits his teeth, banishing any and all thoughts of the monster who rules his life to focus on the girl in front of him. This is the only good thing they have granted him these past three years, and he'll be damned if he lets *her* ruin it.

"Do you want to sit down?" Candi tilts her head, indicating the pile of fabric. "Get a bit more comfortable, maybe?"

He nods stiffly and steps back to reach for them, but she is already kneeling, shaking out blankets and fluffing pillows until they are spread out around her in an oblong circle. *A nest.*

She gives him a slanted smile that suggests she knows exactly what the sight of a woman kneeling amid a such an arrangement of fabric is supposed to do to an alpha. He feels it too, somewhere deep in the parts of him not ruled by engineering: the excitement heating his blood and hardening his cock. But it is... muted. Like he's looking at this pretty little thing through opaque glass, all her bright colors distorted.

"Come." She reaches for him.

He hesitates, then takes it. The shock of *touch* rolls through him again, pulling him down to her. She's still smiling.

AX2 drags his gaze from her painted lips down to her hand, so small and delicate in his. This is what he's longed for for so many endless months. Human connection. Warmth. *Touch.*

He flicks his eyes back up her, pausing at the collar around her neck. Metal clasps wind through a delicate locking mechanism. It looks like something you'd put on a pet. Or a slave.

"You're here voluntarily?" He moves his hand from hers to skim a couple of fingers over the leather.

Her smile tightens as she lowers her lashes. "Mmhm. Unless you'd like to pretend otherwise?"

Something sick and dark twists in his gut and rises like acid up his esophagus. "*No.*"

"A lot of alphas do. I don't mind." Candi teases a fingertip over his where it rests against her collar. He jerks back from the touch without meaning to, making her giggle. "You haven't been with a whore before? The collar's to ensure you don't end up with an accidental mate. We all wear them when we're going to be with an alpha."

A mate.

This time, the horror in his gut is enough to kill the remainders of his erection. He stares down at Candi—at her delicate features and soft body—and imagines what it would be like to be tied to someone so *breakable.* In all the ways he's been broken, his mind could not withstand *that*. He knows it in the marrow of his bones.

"Why are you here?" It comes out gruffer than he means to. *"Offering* yourself to me? You could be hurt." *She* could hurt her.

Candi shrugs, her smile fading some. "This is a pretty safe gig. I've been to military bases before—granted, not blindfolded for three hours while driving there, but they're always well-supervised. And the money's good. Better than normal." She flicks her eyes up to his, the muscles in her face twitching as if she realizes she's let the facade slip. Placing her palm on his chest, she smiles again and says, "Besides... I like the knot. A lot."

She doesn't. He sees the lie in her dark eyes even as she lowers her lashes again and gives him that coy smile expertly crafted to lure him in. He doesn't know her story, but he doesn't need to; three years of forced servitude lets him recognize the desperation that has brought this girl to him. It has nothing to do with desire.

Another flash of the same cursed memory flickers through his mind—a slim neck in his grip, a heavy pulse under his fingers. That haunting moment before he realized the truth of his body's betrayal and allowed *her* scent to roll over his tongue and deep into his lungs. Allowed her to take root in the core of his DNA.

There is no dark undertow to Candi. She's delicate and deliciously curvy, and it would be easy to ignore what's underneath her pretty smiles and take what she's offering. He needs this. *Touch.* Relief.

He grits his teeth and hauls her onto his lap. She giggles, her body pliant as he drapes her over his thighs and crotch. Alive.

"Ooh, you're so strong," she whispers, leaning in against him to press her breasts against his chest. Her breath ghosts over his throat, followed by a flick of her tongue on his Adam's apple that makes him shiver. Slim arms wrap around the back of his neck as she buries her nose against the hollow, inhaling deeply. "Mmm, and you smell good."

She rocks her hips, a slow grind back and forth. Back and forth. Around them, gasps of breath, female whimpers and the sounds of wet flesh speak with all clarity that the other soldiers have had no hesitations in taking what's offered. He shouldn't, either. There is very little light in his existence—precious few moments without despair.

Candi rubs her fingertips against his nape and raises higher until her soft lips press against his ear. "I want your knot, alpha. Please. Make me take it."

No doubt she has been trained to say those words—has learned how to coax an alpha to give in to desire and part with his coin. It doesn't matter.

AX2 groans and tightens his arms around her, burying his nose in her hair and succumbing to the instinctive urge to inhale her pheromones.

A strong scent of vanilla fills his nostrils, layered with peach and a musky hit of pussy—perfume crafted to entice an alpha—but he feels nothing as it fills his lungs.

Slowly, forcing down memories he still refuses to fully acknowledge, he pulls back.

"Is something wrong?" Candi asks, a flicker of genuine concern in her dark eyes.

"No."

She tilts her head, gaze searching. "It's okay if you'd rather just talk. Sometimes that can feel just as good."

He very much doubts that. Even if Dr. Green would allow such a thing.

"Just let me hold you," he says, more softly than he means to.

If she finds the request odd, she doesn't let on. Likely she has encountered far more unusual propositions in her line of work. She sits quietly on his lap, her arms looped loosely around his neck as she watches the other women perform their duties on the scratchy gray blankets.

She feels solid in his arms. Real. AX2 empties his mind and allows himself to simply enjoy the sensation of a woman in his embrace. Of no longer being alone, at least for a little while.

When he closes his eyes, he can almost imagine the scent of floral shampoo in her silky hair.

SIX

ADDIE

The knock on my door is not unexpected ,but it still tightens the knot of dread in my stomach to the point of pain.

I hover in the hallway, hands clenched into fists, as I stare at my front door and force my chest to expand with long, slow breaths.

You knew this was coming, Addie.

Another knock, this time louder. My door vibrates from the force.

"Addie! Enough hiding. Open the door."

My father's voice, muted by the thick wood separating us, but still ringing with authority, cuts through my attempts at calming my nerves. My body reacts before I've given it permission to, taking me the last few steps forward.

Mechanically I raise my hand, unclasp the chain, and slide the lock open with a *click* that rings ominously all the way down to my toes. I don't manage to plaster on the pretense of a smile before my father pushes the door open and steps into my apartment.

"Addie," he rumbles in that tone that always makes me feel like a child again—chiding and vaguely disappointed, but also full of comfort and care. "Seven days? You couldn't answer your phone? Your mother's been worried sick."

I turn around, unable to look him in the eye. He follows my retreat to the living room.

"I'm thirty-three years old, dad. She needs to accept that I don't need her fussing just because I'm off sick for a bit. Besides, it's not like she thought I was dead. I texted her. Twice. Coffee?"

He nods at my offer. "You know how she gets. She wouldn't be able to handle it if something happened to you."

"A stomach bug isn't going to kill me."

When I return with a tray of coffee and cookies—the chocolatey kind my mother doesn't allow him at home—he is sitting on my couch. But rather than relaxing into its plush comfort, he seems to be scanning the room.

Even though I scrubbed every square inch of my space from top to bottom, twice and with bleach, the knot in my stomach still pangs.

"What are you looking for?" I manage with a casual ease I don't feel. I sit on the edge of the armchair facing the couch, the muscles in my back too tense to allow me to lean back.

He flicks his eyes back to me, briefly, before he reaches for a cookie. "A stomach bug, hmm?"

I swallow around a lump in my throat. "Yes, I—"

"Addie." He dunks his cookie once into the coffee—black, no sugar—and lets out a weary sigh. "I watched the security footage from your lab."

There is a ringing in my ears. I can barely focus on it through the sinking feeling traveling down my chest and landing somewhere by my tailbone. "What? W-Why would you—?"

His steely gray eyes flick up to mine again, this time holding my gaze. "Because my only daughter went near-radio silent, and my wife was losing her mind. Is that really what you think we should discuss?"

It sure beats the alternative. I glare at him, because anger is the only shield I can grasp for. "Uh, *yeah*. If a three-star general uses the internal security systems at a government facility to spy on his daughter, I think that warrants some discussion."

My snippy tone merely makes him raise his eyebrows. "Let's not touch on what a three-star general *should* be doing after he witnesses what you did to that man, Addie."

"He's not a goddam *man!*" I snarl, but the rage that flames up through my esophagus is not from his continued dismissal of my repeated explanations that the AX class aren't men. I expect that of him—all he's capable of seeing is the alpha nature remaining.

"Addie." My father puts down his cookie before he folds his hands and sighs again, the sound much like a patient parent indulging their toddler's tantrum. It only infuriates me further.

"Don't!"

"Did he trigger a heat?"

And there it is. I open my mouth to spit out a denial—tell him he is delusional —but the words won't come. It's what I told myself over and over again after I fled the compound that night. All the way home, while my stomach cramped and sweat soaked my car seat and thoughts of *his* hands on me swarmed my mind, and right up until slick flooded my thighs and there was no more refusing the truth.

It took three days before the feverish, agonizing need subsided and my cognitive function returned, flooding me with the horrific truth of what had happened.

"Sweetheart." My father's voice is uncharacteristically soft. "There's no need to be ashamed. I know this isn't something you've ever been interested in, but sometimes nature just takes things into its own hands, hmm? You've spent years on your career. This is only your body reminding you that it's high time you start looking for a husband."

Of course. *Of course* that's his angle. It's been his shitty mantra since before I came of age. I just bet that behind the concerned facade, he's fucking delighted that out of nowhere, my body's decided to commit mutiny. In his primitive brain, it's proof that all his obstinate daughter really needs for eternal happiness is for a big, muscles-for-brains alpha to take her in hand.

In some way, it's almost a relief to return to the familiar argument. As much as it infuriates me, there is comfort in this one known factor amid the scary new reality that I can no longer trust my own body.

I glare at him. "You really believe that, don't you? It doesn't matter that I have spent fifteen *years* on becoming a leading expert in bioengineering—not even when I use that expertise to give *you* the most powerful weapons the U.S. military has seen since the atom bomb. To you, my only true value *still* lies in becoming a broodmare, doesn't it?"

"It's got nothing to do with your value," he sighs. "Your mother and I just want you to be happy, sweetheart. You're a brilliant scientist, but do you really want to keep coming home to this empty apartment every night? What happened between you and that soldier—that's the kind of stuff that can bring you true happiness, if you let it. No one can deny biology, Addie. Not even you."

I suck in a sharp breath when it finally hits me what he's really saying. "Are you *insane?* Are you actually suggesting that because my body reacted when I was *attacked,* it means I'm supposed to give up everything I've worked for to settle down and play housewife? With a *machine?*

"You get that's what he is, right? He's not a human, no matter how much you insist otherwise. I should know— I'm the one who *wired* him. I've welded every inch of metal that keeps his body together. I programmed the chip that controls his entire brain. *Me.* Whatever remains of what he was before is no more than you'd find in any animal. Are you really so desperate to see me married off that literally any alpha who'll sniff in my direction will do?"

My father shakes his head, a sad draw to his mouth. "I'm sorry you see it that way. I'd have hoped experiencing a heat would have softened you, but I guess I should have known better. You've inherited that stubbornness from me, after all."

He stands up and gives me a smile that twists my heart. However much he infuriates me, I hate seeing him upset.

"I've got to get back to your mother."

I nod. "Tell her there's no need to worry about me."

He snorts as he walks to the hallway. "I might as well ask a hurricane to be less windy. She loves you, so she worries. You know that."

I do. I open the door for him with a sigh. "Does she know about... what happened?"

My father gives me a long glance. "I don't keep secrets from her."

Wonderful.

It takes everything I have to force the next question out. "And at work? Dr. Green?"

"Of course not." He hesitates for a moment, then says, "Nevertheless, it would be best if you took some leave, Addie."

I blink. "What?"

"Bluntly, sweetheart, I don't want you near AX2 or the rest of his class before you've gotten a better handle on yourself. Regardless of any... personal issues between you two, he is an extremely valuable asset, and I can't allow any risk to his current training. Social reprogramming is a delicate process, and the kind of punishment you indulged in could ruin our chances for a positive outcome."

"Are you serious? This is my project! You wouldn't have any of these soldiers without me 'indulging' in punishment as part of their training. You can't make me take leave because you disagree with my methods!"

"I can," he says, and there is more of the general than

my loving father in his voice this time. "And I am. Don't force me to go through official channels to do so."

I stare at him, mouth open in shock. He wouldn't. If it became public knowledge that I... that *my body* reacted like it did, I'd never be able to face any of my colleagues again.

The steely look in my father's eyes tells me that yes, he would.

"Leave."

He dips his head in a nod and steps out of my apartment, brushing his hand over my shoulder as he passes.

I go to close the door, but before I can, he turns on my doorstep and looks back at me. "He rejected a woman."

"What?" I hiss, fighting the urge to slam the door on his foot.

"We offered them whores. AX2 didn't indulge. He's the only one. Perhaps something to ponder, seeing how determined you are that he's just a machine. Or a dumb animal." He gives me a small tilt of his lips before he moves off my doorstep and down the stairs.

He's out on the street before my hands stop shaking long enough that I manage to close my door.

TWO DAYS LATER, while I'm curled up on my sofa watching late-night TV with a pint of pity ice cream, a masked man breaks into my apartment.

It's ten days before he sees the other AX models again.

Dr. Green isn't forthcoming with feedback from the session with the prostitutes, but the lack of punishment lets him assume they are not displeased by his refusal to participate. The beta doesn't mention *her* absence, either, his sole focus on pricking needles into AX2's skin and reading test results on the computer.

But on the tenth morning, when Dr. Green enters the lab, he waves two fingers on the hand clutching his usual cup of coffee at AX2. "No need to strip down—we're skipping the tests today. You're scheduled for brunch with the others."

"Brunch?" The concept seems so alien it takes him a moment to connect the word.

"Don't tell me you have an aversion to scrambled eggs

and bacon, as well as willing girls climbing all over you." The beta rolls his eyes and turns back to the door. "We're moving on to the next step of your training. After today's brunch, we will be transferring you into a shared dorm with the other AX soldiers."

His heart gives an odd lurch. "Permanently?"

"So long as things continue to go smoothly, yes. Come on." He walks out the door, leaving AX2 to follow.

An unfamiliar lightness spreads through AX2's chest as the beta's words sink through the humming in his ears. The others... He will be *living* with them? He won't be alone in this lab day after day after day if things go smoothly—and by all the stars in the sky, he will ensure they do—if it means he gets to be with his kin.

He only hesitates for a second, letting his eyes move over the familiar room one last time before he follows Dr. Green.

THE MESS HALL is in another part of the compound he's never seen before. There are several tables and benches set up in the room, and a buffet along the eastern wall. It's unmanned, but the scents of food hit his nostrils the moment he enters.

There are only four occupants—the other AX soldiers. They all look up when he and Dr. Green enter.

"Oi, would you look at that!" Simon grins, a piece of

bacon halfway to his mouth. "Glad you could finally make it, buddy."

"Thought you'd decided to ditch us," Jack says, elbows on the table as he gives AX2 a wide smile. "Grab some food and come sit down."

There is something... off about the scenario playing out in front of him. The last time he saw them, they were as cautious as he—careful not to speak out of turn in front of the doctor. This... This carefree atmosphere doesn't fit with what he knows of this place.

His back muscles flex, tension curling in his gut on instinct, but Dr. Green only nods in the direction of the buffet. "Get yourself a tray. I'll come back at ten to get you settled into the dorm."

AX2 stares mutely after him as the doctor walks out, leaving the five of them alone.

"You really should get in on this before the eggs cool down," Dwayne says between mouthfuls.

AX2 snaps his head back to them. "What the fuck is this?"

His angry rumble makes the others chuckle.

"Yeah, it takes a moment. Welcome to step three of reprogramming. It doesn't come with pussy, but it does have bacon." Sean lifts his chin in the direction of the buffet.

AX2 remains frozen for several long breaths. Experience warns him to be cautious, to expect the other shoe to drop at any moment. His kin's relaxed postures and easy smiles tell another story.

They leave him to work through it, returning their attention to their food and one another.

It takes a few minutes before he forces himself to cross the room, grab a tray and stare at the offered food.

The sheer color of it is overwhelming—the bright yellow of scrambled eggs, reddish brown of bacon, deep green of collards, and vibrant purple of blueberries. Up until now, his meals have consisted of carefully balanced, high-nutrition mush.

When he returns to the table, his tray is loaded five layers high.

"Whoa. You'll be able to eat again later," Simon says, eyebrows lifting as he looks at AX2's tray.

"You're one to talk—you ate thirty fucking oat rolls the first day," Jack snorts. "Leave the man to his food mountain."

"And I was constipated for three days after. Just trying to save his ass—literally," Simon sighs.

"This—how long has this—?" AX2 makes the mistake of biting into a buttered roll of bread, and his question dies on a soft groan. Pure bliss fizzes on his taste buds.

"Since the whores." Sean eyes him carefully. "Next morning, they brought us all here. Everyone except you. We thought maybe the lady doc did something to you."

The memory of soft skin and that throbbing pulse

under his palm pushes at the edges of his mind. He shoves another bite of bread into his mouth, forcing his focus to return to the taste of real food.

"Any idea why they kept you away?" Dwayne asks, his tone slightly too casual. He doesn't quite manage to hide the note of concern.

AX2 only grunts in response.

"Eh. He didn't fuck on command, so they probably just needed to recalibrate his dick." Simon points a fork at him. "Pipes in working order now, bud?"

"Why are they doing this?" AX2 asks around another mouthful of bread. His choice not to answer is deliberate.

Jack shrugs. "Who knows? Something-something training us to act like normies." The smile he cracks doesn't hide the gleam of darkness in his otherwise pale eyes. "Nothing like real food and company to make you forget months of torture and obedience training, eh?"

His tone is sardonic, but AX2 frowns as he takes in his kin. It's only been ten days, but he sees the difference in them. *Reprogramming*, Sean called it. If that's what it is, it looks like it's working.

Every instinct hard-won during his time in this compound tells him that there is something bad coming—that the only reason the scientists in charge would ever allow them this is to have something to take away again later.

It doesn't matter. Even if that's the case—if this will all

be yanked away without warning—he still wants it, *craves* it, with every cell in his body. Just a moment without fear, without loneliness, is worth whatever horrors lie ahead.

BY THE TIME TEN O' clock rolls around, AX2 is full to bursting, and a warm, lethargic sensation threads through his body. It's the best he can remember ever feeling.

When Dr. Green shows up, he leads them to a room with concrete on all four surfaces lit by a single, fluorescent lightbulb. Three bunk beds with gray blankets and gray sheets fill the space, two on either side and one in the middle. Apart from the door they enter through, there's another on the northern wall, undoubtedly leading to the latrine.

"The gym is down the hall on your left," the beta says. "We expect at least five hours a day from you. If your test results drop, we will step in. I suspect you'll prefer it if we don't have to, so put in your best effort. There will be no missions for the time being, but I want you in fighting condition at all times. Understood?"

AX2 nods. His head feels light. They are allowing him control of his day?

Over his body?

"Good. We will be monitoring..." Dr. Green's voice dies when the door behind them bangs open and General Thompson storms through it.

AX2 jerks once, as do the other soldiers, the sudden and aggressive arrival of another alpha sparking instincts not entirely hardwired into compliance.

"General Thompson," Dr. Green begins, his brow furrowing as he catches the look on the other man's face. His lips are pressed into a flat line, but his eyes are wide, their whites pronounced.

"You—AX2. With me," General Thompson snaps, ignoring the doctor as he exits the dorm as swiftly as he entered.

AX2 obeys, his body moving before his mind has fully processed the scene.

General Thompson waits for him in the halls. His posture is staunch, spine arrow-straight and shoulders wide, but the energy emanating off him is jittery and aggressive, and it sparks against AX2's nervous system.

"The Russians have Adelaide," he says the second the door closes behind AX2.

AX2 blinks. "What?" The question is out of his mouth before his training kicks in. He braces for the sear of his chip, but the general is far too agitated to punish him for the slip.

"They kidnapped her. The commie bastards took my daughter right from under my *fucking* nose. I've managed to locate her whereabouts—they're holding her in a bunker in Eastern Siberia." He pulls his fingers through his short hair and turns to AX2. "I need you to get her back."

A roil of emotions heats his gut—confusion and dread most prominent. He is careful to keep his voice monotone when he says, "I have not been trained for search and rescue, sir."

General Thompson rounds on him, his steel-gray eyes narrowing to a glare. "I don't give a shit. If I take this through the proper channels, and if she's..." He sucks in a sharp breath, jaw clenching around whatever he was about to say. "You're the best I've got. And I am ordering you to rescue my daughter. Save her, no matter the cost."

He is dropped in a barren, snow-covered wasteland on the Eurasian continent. *Eastern Siberia* is all the information he's been given. Usually he has exact coordinates and detailed instructions of when, where, and how. Not this time.

Save her. This is the only command he's been given, but there are precious few details on the opposition he will face. *They're in a bunker,* he's been told. *Five-to-twenty men, likely heavily armed.*

He pushes his frustration down as he jogs through the waist-high drifts, his weapon at the ready, hunched over to brace against the howling winds throwing blinding flurries into his face. None of it matters; he's been given a mission, and he will see it through. His chip will make sure of it.

Even if he hopes he finds her dead.

. . .

HE LOCATES the bunker two hours in.

A shoddy-looking barbed wire fence surrounds the concrete structure only barely visible amid the rocky terrain. It blends in almost perfectly with the bumpy, white landscape, but he spots the singular guard by the entrance. A semi-automatic is in his hand, but his focus is scattered, likely from the biting cold.

AX2 has his knife at the guard's throat before the man realizes he's not alone in the freezing wilderness.

"How many?" he snarls, pressing the blade deeper when the soldier jumps.

"Der'mo!" the guard spits.

"How many?" AX2 repeats.

"Fifty. American pig."

AX2 clasps a palm over the man's mouth and slides his knife across his throat. The guard jerks once, a wet rattle escaping through AX2's fingers before he slumps

The heavy steel door to the bunker is secured by a fingerprint scanner. AX2 yanks the dead soldier's glove off and pushes his hand to the screen, waiting for the beep of the lock before he tosses the corpse aside.

There are eight men in the bunker, not fifty.

They are all armed, but they aren't expecting a fight—and they certainly aren't expecting *him*.

It takes AX2 seconds to kill the first six—one inside

the corridor, and the other five when he moves into the first room, which looks to be the kitchen and common area. He shoots three more men dead before the remaining two are on their feet, guns drawn.

One of them manages to fire off a round, but AX2 twists out of the way before it impacts. He puts a bullet between his attacker's eyes, ducks another shot, leaps across the room, and thrusts his knife into the remaining man's chest, all the way to the hilt.

The soldier gurgles, his hand spasming around his gun, but he doesn't have enough strength left to pull the trigger. When he slides to the floor, AX2 is already turning to the door, beyond which shouts and the sound of running feet echo.

He shoots the first man the second he hurdles through the door, but the second manages to jerk back before he takes a bullet to the temple.

This one is bigger than the other men—the only alpha present—yet he isn't wearing the same kind of combat gear as the rest of the soldiers. He is wearing a thick sweater and jeans, but he's holding the gun in his hand as if he knows how to use it.

AX2 doesn't wait to find out. He leaps across the room again, back to the door, lifts his weapon, and fires it into the man's chest.

The moment the first bullet bites into the other alpha, a scream rings from deeper in the bunker. It's muted by concrete walls and steel doors, but the agony in it deafens him.

The enemy alpha only lets out a soft gasp, his eyes widening as if he can't quite believe his own defeat. Then they turn glassy. He sinks to his knees, his hands falling limply to his sides, gun clattering to the floor.

By the time his head hits the concrete, he's already gone.

Another scream rips through the bunker—a wail so primal and animalistic it doesn't sound human. But it is.

Save her.

AX2 is moving before he has made the conscious connection between that wail and the doctor he's here to rescue, his chip's impulses impossible to resist.

There is only one door at the end of the dark hallway, made of thick steel.

Readying his gun, he tries the handle. Locked.

"Step away from the door," he shouts, aiming his weapon at the lock.

The shot is deafening, but it works. The lock blows out of the steel door, clanking to the floor. AX2 moves swiftly, kicking open the door and scanning the room for enemies.

But there is only *her*.

Doctor Adelaide Thompson kneels on an unmade bed. Her dark hair is wild, her usually pale, impassive face red and blotchy and drawn in a silent scream, and those cold, gray eyes he loathes so much are wide and unfocused without her glasses, overflowing with tears.

During the years he's spent in her lab, she has shown him nothing but blank indifference, an unfeeling facade—sparks of irritation at most. His tormentor calls him a machine, but in the privacy of his mind, that is how he thinks of *her*: a cold, mechanical entity. Impersonal.

Inhuman.

The woman in front of him now... The pain and terror on her face is the most human thing he has ever seen.

She is naked. It takes a moment to register.

In her lab, he has always awakened in the stasis chamber nude. She has always worn a white lab coat, the absence of his clothing and the presence of hers a stark reminder of his status as something less than a person.

There is no mistaking the monster who has tortured him for so many years. Yet the sight of her, like *this*, stripped of her dignity and that cold, impenetrable facade...

She finally seems to notice his presence and chokes out an awful, rasping sob. "Help... Help me..."

Save her.

AX2 enters the room, his intent to retrieve her and fulfill his mission. But before he reaches the bed, his gaze catches on the streaks of blood dripping from her ribcage. She's clawing at it, tearing bloody strips in her own skin.

Something flickers at the back of his mind, making his

strides falter before he reaches her—a ghost of what might have been a memory, but there is nothing but darkness.

The red of her blood is nearly obscene against her pale skin. It trickles sluggishly over the finger-shaped bruises on her hips. Catches on the crusty, iridescent streaks marring her belly and thighs.

"Please. Please, help me." Her voice breaks even as she hooks her fingers and claws at her own flesh. Digging.

There is no saving her. He knows it in his gut even before he reaches for her hair and twists her head to the side, displaying the deep indents of teeth left there.

Her claiming mark.

She has been claimed. And her alpha...

He lies dead down the hall.

The woman in front of him erased much of what he was, but there are a few precious things that even she could never take. Less than human as he is, he is still all alpha. And his alpha instincts recognize the meaning of that mark on a level that runs deeper than his DNA.

Her captor bonded her to him. Made her a part of him. Now that he's dead, she will die too.

Save her.

AX2 bares his teeth against the impulse from his chip. He grabs her wrists to stop her attempt at digging out her pair-bond despite the futility of doing so.

She gasps another sob, struggling weakly to resume ripping at her own flesh, and he growls as his chip fires painfully.

Save her. Save her. Save her.

"It hurts," she whimpers. "It *hurts!* Make it stop. Please, *please* make it stop!"

He stares down at the woman he hates more than he will ever hate anyone or anything else—and feels a thread of pity worm its way through his gut. He didn't know he was capable of such emotion, let alone for *her*. But as she sits in front of him, so fundamentally broken he knows nothing will ever be able to glue her back together again, something aches in his chest.

"I can't," he says.

Her breathing stutters and a fresh bout of tears floods down her cheeks. But when she looks to his side, to his gun, a whisper of steel echoes in the determination crossing her features. "Yes, you can."

AX2 inhales sharply. His orders are to save her, and the fundamental parts of his wiring have been programmed to never allow him to hurt her. The chip sears his brain at the thought of giving her what she asks for, and he remembers the feeling of her throat in his hand. How he couldn't bring himself to snap her neck, no matter how much he wanted to.

He repeats, *"I can't."*

"I command you!" Her high-pitched voice rings with desperation. "Stop the pain. Whatever you have to do, just fucking stop it! That's an order, AX2."

The command burns through his nervous system, his

fingers twitching against her wrists. Her demand conflicts with his previous orders, manifesting as an excruciating sizzle in his chip.

If he obeys her, he will die too. The realization is sudden and sharp on the wave of agony.

Icy exhilaration runs up his spine. *Death.* He has longed for it, only to be denied over and over. *She* has denied him, forcing him back from the relief of nothingness more times than he can count. But now?

One flick of his finger, and he'll be free. His death won't be easy, won't be clean. Disobeying orders will be maddening. But he is not afraid of pain; *she* has made sure of that. And he will go to his grave knowing that in the end, he took her life, just as she took his.

Which seems a far more satisfying end than he could have ever hoped for.

AX2 releases her wrists and steps back. When he grabs for his weapon, the agony in his brain nearly blinds him, but he still presses the barrel of his gun to her forehead.

Her breathing quickens, her sobs pitching higher as she squeezes her eyes shut.

He has killed so many times before. She has given the order for most of them on the orders of someone else. They are both cogs in the same machine.

He stares down at her tear-stricken face and the wild,

dark hair he has only seen smoothed back and tight against her skull before.

She has been here for days. She has been at that now-dead alpha's mercy for *days*, and the proof of what has been done to her during that time is caked to her skin and smeared over the sheets beneath her.

Perhaps she has longed for death for some time.

"*God,*" she croaks. "Please!"

God. He doesn't know if he has ever believed in God, or heaven. He certainly doesn't now, and hearing *her* use that word is startling. But there is no god here, and no salvation. Only him.

His finger twitches on the trigger.

Save her.

The image flashes through his brain on the tail-end of the command—a flimsy, unbidden vision: His lips against the scabbed-over scar on her neck. His teeth digging in. The taste of her blood spilling into his mouth and the sensation of iron hooks burrowing into his heart.

There is *one* way to save her.

His gun slips from his hand and clatters to the ground as he jolts back, away from the bed.

No. No, no, no!

But it's too late. He doesn't know what nightmare the knowledge comes from—what deeply buried instinct forced its way to the surface before he could take his freedom, or why it has—but he can't unknow it now.

His ragged breath shudders out of his lungs as he stares down at the monster who has broken him beyond the bounds of humanity.

There *is* a way to save a woman from the loss of her alpha—he must replace her broken bond with another.

TEN

AX2

Save her.

No. Stars above, *no!*

AX2's eyes are wide as he stares down at the broken woman before him, his heart thumping fast and unevenly behind his ribs. He can't wrap his mind around the concept, but it's there, no matter how hard he tries to make it disappear.

If he mates her—if he claims her as his—she will survive. He knows it in the marrow of his bones.

His chip fires angrily through his brain, the command like a hammer rather than a spike, now that he sees a way to obey both sets of orders. It urges him on, zinging against his nervous system with the demand to *save her. Make her pain stop.*

If he does this, she will be a part of him in ways far

more horrific, far more intimate, than what she has done to him before. The very last vestiges of his mind will be hers too.

No. Not this. This he can't do. He won't.

AX2 bends for his gun, but his fingers slip on the metal and he stumbles forward, only barely catching himself against the bed.

Shit. He tries again, but the shock of the chip turns his vision white.

He can't kill her now that he knows that doing so isn't saving her. He missed his chance.

"Fuck!" he snarls, the fury in his voice making the woman whimper and withdraw.

His sight fades back into focus, and he sees her cowering on the bed as far away from him as she can get. Only then does he notice the manacle around her right ankle chaining her to the bed, and the raw, bleeding skin underneath it. She fought for her freedom.

Not all females do. Most will capitulate underneath an alpha. She did not.

She will fight beneath him too.

With mechanical movements, he straightens. Her eyes go round when he reaches for his belt.

"W-What are you doing? Stop!"

His muscles lock up, his fingers twitching against the buckle as his chip sears with another constricting command. *Shit.* His chip is still calibrated to obey her commands, but the roar of the general's orders throb through his brain.

Save her. Save her.

"You want to die?" he grits. He grabs the gun from the floor, unhindered now that his intentions are no longer to kill her, and tosses it on the bed. "Then take your own life. I can't do it for you. But... I can make the pain stop."

She stares at him, uncomprehending, her breath coming in quick gasps. Her fingers still move against her bleeding ribs, digging. "What?"

"The only way to heal a broken mate-bond is to replace it with another," he growls. "It's that, or you die. Your call."

Her mouth opens and closes, but no sound comes out. He can see her desperation to deny him—it's written all over her harrowed face. She wants this as little as he does, and he hopes with everything he is that she will surrender to death. His chip might kill him if he lets her die, but death does not scare him.

Especially not when the alternative is *her.*

She stares at him for several shaky breaths, eyes flicking to his gun for several more. His heart drops to his gut when steely resolution settles over her pale features, lending her the illusion of her former strength.

"If... If that's what it takes. Do it."

Without another look at him, she turns on the bed, presenting him with her naked back. Her left hand is still pressed against her wound, her right clutching the stained bedding.

AX2 lets out a low breath, the relief when his chip no longer fires conflicting orders at him nearly enough to drown out the anger boiling his bones.

Nearly.

This damnable woman—this cruel *cunt*—has taken everything from him, and now, she demands *this* too? His fucking *claim?* She, who doesn't even see him as human?

But of course. To her, he is nothing but a weapon, a tool. Something to be used. Only this time... This time, he gets to use her too.

He kneels on the bed and grabs her hair, yanking her up higher on her knees before he pushes her forward, forcing her to brace against the bed on both elbows. She's stiff in his grasp, every muscle in her shaking body tensed to the point of snapping, and when he lifts a knee to spread her thighs apart, she whimpers.

But she doesn't fight him.

His breath is labored as he pulls back to free his cock, anger hardening his body in place of any real desire for what lies ahead. He has fantasized about hurting her countless times, about breaking her body apart until her heart stops beating, but never like this.

The realization makes him pause as his gaze slides over her back and hips, covered in purple bruises from where she's been used before.

It shouldn't matter—he gets to hurt her now, like she has him so many times before. Fuck, she's even commanded him to.

Only it's... not the same.

It doesn't matter. Only her pain should matter.

It *is* the only thing that matters.

He bares his teeth and grabs her by the scruff again, pushing her face into the dirty mattress. His free hand he places between her barely parted thighs, pressing up against her pussy to spread her. Her skin is cold.

She jolts against his touch, twitching as if she wants to close her legs, but she doesn't. She stays put, even as her quiet sobs make her tremble.

She is dry. Dry and tight, and the stench of the other alpha soaks the sheets and her marred skin. When he brushes over something crusty, she yelps and jerks hard.

AX2 glances down. Powdery blood dusts his fingertips. The scab he has unwittingly rubbed against bleeds a little, coloring a thin strip of her pink flesh scarlet. It isn't the only wound there—maybe half a dozen minor tears are scabbed over around her opening.

His heart gives an odd sort of *thump* low in his chest at the proof of what, exactly, has been done to her. It should bring him joy—to know that his tormentor found someone even more monstrous than she is.

It doesn't.

Silently he pulls away, releasing her neck in the process.

She doesn't move, and he can still hear her shallow sobs as he pushes off the bed and searches the room for something that might make him come out of this with even a shred of his soul intact.

Funny. Up until this very moment, he didn't think he had any soul left to shred. He was sure she stole the last remnants of it long ago.

There's a bottle of machine lubricant on a dusty shelf. Translucent mineral oil. Not ideal, but better than nothing.

He returns to the bed where she still lays, unmoving. Legs apart. Waiting to be *saved*.

His cock is soft and reluctant to rise, and the sight of her bruised body does little to entice it. Even the anger that had him hard before is gone.

AX2 closes his eyes and gives his dick a slow pump. It barely twitches.

Save her.

He's fucking trying.

An unbidden image flickers at the back of his mind—the same picture he has used before, in the privacy of her lab late at night. Of *her*—not the broken little thing crumpled on the bed, but the cold, cruel woman he hates with everything he is. Her surprising warmth as she brushes a hand over his naked chest. The floral scent of her shampoo.

His cock swells, and he bites back a groan of loathing.

Curse it all to goddamn hell.

Unbidden, his free hand finds the curve of her hip. She stiffens under his palm again, to the point he doesn't know how she avoids snapping a tendon, but he doesn't grab her. The soft feel of her skin, of *touch,* is more than enough, and he keeps his eyes closed around the image of the many times she has examined him.

He pumps his cock faster, swallowing another groan as it starts to feel good, and the image of her twists into that night after his first meeting with the others. Of her warm throat against his palm, her heavy pulse. Her scent filling his lungs as he breathed her in.

"Fuck!" He bites out the curse and wrenches his eyes open to the harsh light of reality, but this time, the sight of her vulnerable and defeated does nothing to quell the need pulsing through his cock.

He keeps his hand on her hip as he grabs for the bottle of lubricant, flicks it open with his thumb, and squirts it onto her soft flesh.

She whimpers when he follows the liquid with a finger, dipping it deep to ensure the oil reaches every-where it needs to. The squeeze of her muscles protesting the intrusion has his cock throbbing.

"Shh. I'm not gonna hurt you," he hears himself say—a bold-faced lie. "I don't want to hurt you."

Another lie; he wants to hurt her with every fiber of his being, just... not like this.

She makes a mewling sound—like a scared kitten pinned and pleading for mercy—and *shit*, he wishes it didn't make his cock jump.

"Okay. Just breathe, girl. It'll be over soon."

He brings the head of his throbbing member to her slickened opening, and her sobs turn to hyperventilation, her hands fisting in the sheets.

There is no point in drawing it out.

"*Ow!*" Her scream rips through the room, her body jerking to expel him.

Shit!

He slips his hand from her hip around her stomach and anchors her in place as she turns wild beneath him, instincts she can do nothing to control flaring to life.

Her skin is so cold everywhere she presses against him with her bucking, her hair smells like sour sweat and sex, and the slick clench of her muscles as he fills her sends lightning through his nerves. It's sickening—and it's fucking ecstasy.

"You're okay. You're okay." He gasps the empty promise against her ear with every thrust, her desperate screams squeezing his gut as tightly as her pussy's clasp on his cock. *Shit*, he hates how fucking good she feels.

His body has no ambivalence. It's a mercifully short while before he senses the swelling at the bottom of his shaft. *Thank fuck.*

She feels it too, and her fighting turns downright feral. "Not that! Not that! No, no, no, *no!*"

"Shh," he groans, tightening his grip around her until she feels like a part of his own body. *"Fuck!* I have to do this. It's the only way."

She lets out a whimper, caging her protests behind gritted teeth. And then he feels her hand against his arm bracing them on the bed. She grabs on so tight her knuckles turn white.

"Do it," she says.

He doesn't need her permission, but her hoarse whisper sends lightning up his spine nonetheless.

"Oh, *fuck!*"

His knot swells fast, stretching her wide, and her whimpering turns even more desperate—more pained.

He doesn't think; reacting on instinct alone, he reaches for her clit with his oil-slick fingers. He falls down on top of her, keeping her pinned to the mattress as he slowly works his still-swelling knot through her protesting sheath.

"Shit! Shit! Shit!" Her cursing is high-pitched and panicked, but he feels her flutter around his cock every time he strokes her nub until—*fuck!*—her pussy snaps shut around the bottom of his knot like a damn elastic band,

and all he sees are stars. Everything is hot, pulsing flesh—
and utter euphoria.

Save her.

Her nape is clammy from their combined sweat, and
rich with her pheromones. He sucks in greedy lungfuls
and groans when his balls draw up tight, until, *finally...!*

He has never known release like this—never known
anything could give him such complete and perfect *relief.*

Without thought for the consequences, AX2 bites
down on his tormentor's neck, breaking her skin and
reopening the fresh scar left by her first alpha.

A single word pounds in his brain, reverberating
through his body and into the very helix of his DNA:

Mine.

TREACHERY

CONTINUE AX2'S STORY IN TREACHERY:

Her unwilling protector. His unwilling mate.

I created him. Put him back together when he was nothing but ripped muscle and snapped bones.

I made him stronger. Faster. Lethal. I molded him into a weapon. And for three years, I controlled his every breath.

He hates me for it.

I hate him, too.

When I was weak and desperate and thought I would die, he was the one who came for me.

He claimed my freedom to save my life, and I am no longer the one in control.

Now, he is my unwilling protector, and I...

I am his unwilling mate.

ALSO BY NORA ASH

PROTECTOR

Rage

Treachery

Bound

ALPHA TIES

Alpha

Feral

THE OMEGA PROPHECY

Ragnarök Rising

Weaving Fate

Betraying Destiny

DEMON'S MARK

Branded

Demon's Mark

Prince of Demons

ANCIENT BLOOD

Origin

Wicked Soul

Debt of Bones*

DARKNESS

Into the Darkness

Hidden in Darkness

Shades of Darkness

Fires in the Darkness

MADE & BROKEN

Dangerous

Monster

Trouble